WONDER DOG

PB
F
SC U

Have you read these Shooting Star books?

- ❏ *Aliens in the Basement* • Suzan Reid
- ❏ *The Big Race!* • Sylvia McNicoll
- ❏ *A Ghost in the Attic* • Suzan Reid
- ❏ *Howard's House is Haunted* • Maureen Bayless
- ❏ *Liar, Liar, Pants on Fire* • Gordon Korman
- ❏ *The Lost Locket* • Carol Matas
- ❏ *Monsters in the School* • Martyn Godfrey
- ❏ *Princesses Don't Wear Jeans* • Brenda Bellingham
- ❏ *Project Disaster* • Sylvia McNicoll
- ❏ *School Campout* • Becky Citra
- ❏ *Sleepover Zoo* • Brenda Kearns
- ❏ *Starring Me!* • Cathy Miyata
- ❏ *Worm Pie* • Beverly Scudamore

WONDER DOG

Beverly Scudamore

Illustrations by
Susan Gardos

Scholastic Canada Ltd.

Canadian Cataloguing in Publication Data

Scudamore, Beverly, 1956–
  Wonder dog

ISBN 0-590-51874-7

I. Title.

PS8587 C82W66 2000   jC813'.54   C99-932319-9
PZ7.S38Wo 2000

5 4 3 2 1   Printed in Canada   0 1 2 3 4/0

Contents

1. Puppy Love. 1

2. Sour Grapefruit. 8

3. Oh, Brother!. 15

4. Fur and Feathers. 21

5. One Strange Bird. 28

6. My Dog Is Better Than Your Dog 36

7. A Surprise Visitor 42

8. Big Trouble 49

9. Tricks 'n' Treats. 56

10. Rags Goes to School 65

11. Friends to the Rescue 73

12. And the Winner Is 77

For Kristine.

Chapter 1

Puppy Love

I wanted a dog. That's all. Lots of kids have dogs — so I didn't think it was a big deal.

Boy, was I wrong!

The trouble started last summer when Sassy, the Andersons' golden retriever, had puppies. Twelve! When the puppies were born, they were just a handful of fur. They couldn't hear or see until they were ten days old. But puppies grow fast. By the fall, they were big enough to leave their mother. And they were for sale at the end of my street.

My mission: to get one of the puppies.

Monday morning, I knocked on Amy Matola's door. She lives across the street and three houses over. She was still in her red, stretchy pyjamas when she answered the door. That didn't bother her. We've been friends since kindergarten.

"Hi, Kirbs," she said, "Why are you here . . . and so early? I usually pick *you* up."

"You've got to help me," I moaned. "The Andersons sold another puppy yesterday. Now there are only seven."

We ran up to Amy's bedroom and closed the door. I fell back on her bed. "Do you believe in love at first sight?"

Amy tossed her pyjamas onto the bedpost. "In your case, it's 'love at first bite.' "

I glanced at the red tooth marks on my arm. "Puppies need to chew."

Amy cracked up. "I guess that makes you

a human teething ring."

I sat up. "How am I going to get a puppy? My parents said no."

"Begging didn't work?" she asked, struggling into her jeans.

"Nope. Just put them in a worse mood."

"Why don't you do something to impress them?" Amy suggested. "Parents love it when kids act responsible."

"That's it!" I cried. "I know exactly what to do. Amy, you're the best!" I headed for the door. "Let's go!"

"Wait. I haven't brushed my hair yet."

"Your hair looks awesome," I said. And it did. The only way I can make my hair go that kinky is if I sleep in braids.

"Okay," she laughed. "I can't find my brush anyway."

On the way out, Amy stopped to make sure Josephine had water. Hanging upside down from the top of the cage, the hamster poked her little pink nose through the metal bars. "We'll play later," Amy promised. "You're supposed to sleep in the daytime, silly."

"Hurry," I said, "or we'll miss all the fun."

Amy's eyes lit up. "Fun? What fun?"

"You'll see."

Amy could hardly keep up as I raced down the sidewalk. I slowed down in front of the Andersons' house.

"Not the puppies again," she grumbled.

"Come on!" I grabbed her hand. "Don't be a party pooper."

She dug her heels into the ground. "We visited the puppies yesterday, and then we were late for school. You know what will happen if we're late again. Besides, I can't wait to find out why Miss Santos asked us to bring spoons for science."

Amy spotted Jill Abram at the corner. She ran to catch up to her — and I ran into the Andersons' backyard.

Sassy was asleep beside her doghouse. Stretched out in the morning sunlight, she looked like a golden lioness.

"Hi, Sass," I said, crouching beside her.

The puppies were at the other end of the yard, jumping and snapping at the air, trying to catch a white moth. Suddenly, one spotted me and came running. The rest followed.

"Puppy attack!" I cried, ducking behind Sassy.

Sassy made a great, furry wall. But the puppies still found me. All seven pounced on me. *Arf! Arf! Arf!* They yanked at my ponytail, tickled my neck, climbed up my back, tugged at my shoelaces.

I scrambled to my feet. Time for my secret weapon. I reached into my backpack and pulled out my red ball.

"Fetch!" I cried, tossing the ball across the yard.

Six puppies chased after the ball. The seventh one stayed behind, whimpering at my feet, so I scooped her up in my arms.

"What's up, Fuzzy-Wuzzy?"

This puppy looked different from the rest. Golden curls swirled into a little tornado on top of her head. She looked up at me with big,

brown eyes . . . and sank her teeth into my arm.

"Quit it!" I laughed. "I'm not a chew toy!"

Mrs. Anderson stuck her head out the back door. "Kirby, dear, doesn't the bell ring at nine o'clock?"

"Huh?" I checked my watch. 8:58 AM. "Uh-oh, got to go." I put the puppy down, then stuffed my hair back into a ponytail holder and rushed out the gate.

The bell rang. School was still a whole block away.

I broke into a run. The Willow Elementary sign came into sight. "I'm going to make it, I'm going to — Oooff!"

Wipeout! The puppies had undone my laces.

I skidded into class during morning announcements. Miss Santos was reading a note at her desk. Her long, dark hair had fallen over her eyes. She didn't notice me.

Yes. A lucky break.

Chapter 2

Sour Grapefruit

After *O Canada*, Miss Santos put half a grapefruit on each desk. "Take out your spoons," she instructed the class. "You may begin eating."

Jared Jones stuck his hand in the air. "Miss Santos, I already ate breakfast."

"This isn't breakfast," she said. "This is science."

"Oh, in that case . . . " He jabbed his spoon

into the grapefruit, took a bite and shouted, "Pucker power!"

Everyone — even Miss Santos — started to laugh.

The grapefruit made a big mess. They kept sliding around the desks and wiping out on the floor. The juice sprayed everywhere. Miss Santos was not laughing anymore. In fact, her face had turned a little sour.

"When you are finished," she said, "place the grapefruit skins on the table at the back of the room. Once they dry out, we will use them to make bird feeders."

Craig Gilbert turned in his chair and made a face at me. "Bird feeders out of the grapefruit skin? Weird!" He plunked a grapefruit half upside down on his head and crossed his eyes. "Hello, I am Mr. Grapefruit Head."

"Craig," Miss Santos called from across the room. "Take that off your head!"

Craig lifted it off. Pulp and juice had soaked his buzz cut.

"Ha ha!" I laughed. "You got slimed!"

Miss Santos walked over to my desk. Uh-oh.

"Kirby, I need to speak with you."

"But, Miss Santos, I couldn't help laughing. Craig's hair — "

"This isn't about Craig," she said firmly. "You were late for school again today. I will have to send a note home."

She *had* seen me!

"No! I mean . . . I couldn't help it."

"Why is that?" she asked.

"Ummm . . . " Think fast, think fast, think fast! " . . . on the way to school, my spoon fell out of my backpack. It got covered with mud and ants and stuff . . . so I cleaned it in the girls' washroom."

It was one little lie — for a good reason.

Miss Santos stared at me. My face got hot. My stomach went *squish*.

"I'm glad you found your spoon, Kirby," she said finally. "Please, make sure you are not late for school tomorrow."

"Yes, Miss Santos," I answered, looking down at my desk.

When Miss Santos had returned to her desk, I dug into my grapefruit. At the same time, a hand tugged on my ponytail. Grapefruit juice squirted up my nose. I turned and glared.

"Amy told me the real reason why you were late," Miranda Simpkins whispered.

"So? It's none of your business." I turned back to face the front.

"Mom and I went to the Andersons' house last night," she went on. "I got to choose a puppy of my very own."

I whirled around. "Which one?"

"The most beautiful one. Her fur is honey-coloured, and it's curly on top — just like my hair." She ran her fingers through her hair, fluffing it up.

My hands curled into fists. "You can't have that puppy! She's mine!"

"Is not."

"Is too! I'm going to get my parents to buy that puppy tonight."

Miranda grinned. "Too late. My mom already paid for her."

"LIAR!" I yelled, forgetting I was at school.

Miss Santos clapped her hands hard. "Kirby Carson! Turn and face the front."

When the class had finished slurping up grapefruit, it was time for gym. I grabbed my sweatshirt and headed to the soccer field.

Miss Santos divided the class into two teams. Then the game began.

Jared dribbled the ball past me to Jill. She booted the ball to Miranda. I darted up the field to block Miranda. Then *whomp!* I hit the ground hard.

When I looked up, I saw Miranda staring down at me. Her mouth was wide open. I counted three fillings.

"Are you okay?" she asked.

"You tripped me," I roared.

"Did not."

"Did too."

"Can't prove it."

"So what? I quit!"

I limped off the field and dropped to the

ground under a large willow tree. Amy came running after me. "Kirbs, are you okay? We need you on our team."

"Not if Miranda is playing. She cheats. Did you see her trip me?"

"Well, no," Amy admitted, "but I wasn't looking."

Miss Santos called from the sideline. "Kirby, are you all right?"

"Guess so," I said, rubbing my knee.

"Back in the game, then. You too, Amy."

"Don't let Miranda bug you," Amy said, as we headed back to the field.

"I can't help it. Miranda's getting the puppy I want. She gets everything."

"I don't understand," Amy said. "You two used to be friends."

"Yeah, well, that was before she bought the last green rocket yo-yo at Smith's Toy Mart. She knew how much I wanted that yo-yo."

"Did she do it on purpose?"

"YES! And it's the same thing with the puppy."

"So pick another puppy," Amy said. "They're all cute."

"But I don't want any old puppy. I want the puppy with the curls on top!"

Suddenly, I remembered my plan to impress Mom and Dad. I jabbed the air with a karate kick.

Miranda didn't have the puppy yet. Maybe it wasn't too late!

Chapter 3

Oh, Brother!

"Quack, quack, quackquackquackquack . . . "
I plugged my ears.

" . . . quackquackquack." Marcus ran through the kitchen, dragging Ducky behind him. The wheels of his pull toy were spinning in the air. The duck's head was going *whack, whack, whack* on the floor. Susan, our babysitter, was yelling, "Stop! Stop! Stop!"

Marcus is my little brother. He is three years

old, but he acts like a big baby. His hair is cut in the shape of a bowl. He has brown freckles and skin the colour of milk. Put it all together, and he looks like an upside-down bowl of Krispy Rice cereal.

Marcus dropped the duck. He grabbed my hand and pulled me to the kitchen table. "Look, I coloured my bestest picture for you."

"Cool!" I said, staring at the red, blue and green scribble. "What is it?"

"Me and you holding hands."

"Thought so. Just checking. That is awesome blue hair you gave me." I hit him with a high-five. "Why don't you draw Mom and Dad a picture?" I suggested. "How about a puppy? They would love that."

Marcus smiled. "A gween puppy." He picked up a green crayon and began to scribble. And I ran to my bedroom.

When my parents got home from work, Dad read Marcus a book about wild animals while Mom started dinner.

"Dad," I said, breaking into the story. "I

have one question. Then I won't bother you anymore."

He looked up from the book and smiled. "What's up, kiddo?"

This was my big chance. I took a deep breath. "Can I get one of the Andersons' puppies? Can I, can I? Huh, huh? . . . OH, PLEEEEEASE!"

Dad's smile disappeared. His eyes went back to the book. "Not now, Kirby."

"You mean, I can get one later — after dinner?"

"I mean, I don't want to talk about it now."

"Okay, Dad, I'll wait until it's a good time."

I sat quietly until Dad finished reading the story. Then I announced: "Ladies and gentlemen, time for a big surprise!"

I grabbed Mom and Dad by the hand and made them follow me to my bedroom.

"Wow!" Dad exclaimed. "It's clean!"

Mom gave me a hug. "I'm glad you have finally decided to take care of your room," she said.

"Now that I'm eight years old, I can take care of lots of things," I told them. With any luck, they got the message.

At supper, Mom turned into an airplane. "Zoom, zoom! Open wide! Here comes Mr. Speedy!"

Marcus's mouth clamped shut. Mom tried the airplane game a few more times. Marcus refused to open his mouth. After a while, she put down the spoonful of meat loaf. Marcus picked the peas off his plate and shoved them into his mouth.

Finally, it was quiet. Now or never, I told myself.

"I visited the puppies today," I began. "One is extra cute. She has little curls on the top of her head, and she's the size of a bunny. But, of course, she'll get tons bigger — just like Sassy. Can I get that puppy? Can I, can I? Huh, huh? . . . OH, PLEEEEEASE!"

Mom put her fork down. "Kirby, do you remember what happened when we visited the Andersons last week?"

"Uh . . . I played with Sassy?"

She reminded me about the rest: "Marcus chased Sassy in circles trying to grab her tail. He climbed on her back and rode her like a horse. When Mrs. Anderson pulled Marcus off her, he had clumps of Sassy's fur in each hand."

"Don't worry, Mom," I said. "I'll keep the puppy away from Marcus. Besides, if I don't rescue her, Miranda is going to get her. And she's even worse than Marcus."

"Sorry, Kirby," Dad said. "A dog doesn't make sense right now. Perhaps when Marcus is a little older . . ."

"How about a hamster or a gerbil?" Mom suggested. "That way you can keep your pet safe in a cage."

"I don't want a hamster! I don't want a gerbil! I want — "

Crash! Bang!

Dad jumped up from the table. "What was that?"

Dad and I ran to the front yard, just in time to see our garbage pail rolling on its side . . . and an animal disappearing around the side of the neighbour's house.

Chapter 4

Fur and Feathers

The next morning Amy picked me up for school. This time I didn't visit the puppies. I couldn't risk being late again. Lying to Miss Santos had turned my stomach upside down — kind of like the time I ate all my Halloween candy in one night.

We started the day with science. Everyone gathered at the back of the room.

"First we will make bird feeders," Miss

Santos said. She handed out pencils and string.

Using the pointed end of the pencils, we poked four little holes around the top of the grapefruit. Then we threaded string through the holes and tied a knot at the ends.

"Now I get it," Craig said, swinging a feeder from his fingers. "Awesome. Even better than a hat."

"Find a partner," Miss Santos said. "I want each group to fill one feeder with fatty bird cake and one with bird chow."

She brought out a bucket of birdseed and a bag of suet, which is beef fat, she told us. Ew! Amy and I worked together. Making fatty bird cake was gooey and fun. We just mixed a ball of suet with a handful of seeds. Then we dumped the strange looking cake into a grapefruit skin.

Things got pretty weird when it was time to make bird chow. Miss Santos brought out a box of dog bones and a bag filled with brown eggshells.

I raised my hand. "Miss Santos, why are some eggs white and some brown?"

"It depends on the breed of hen," she explained. "But whether the eggs are brown or white on the outside, they are all the same on the inside."

I placed my creamy white hand next to Amy's golden-brown hand. "Just like us," I said, sealing it with a high-five.

To make bird chow, we crushed up dog bones and eggshells with a rolling pin. Then we dumped the crumbs into a grapefruit skin.

Jared raised his hand. "Feeding eggshells to birds is mean. The birds will choke."

"Yeah," Jill piped up. "And if dog bones are really meant for birds, shouldn't they be called bird bones?"

Miss Santos clasped her hands together. "I love it when students ask questions! As part of our wild bird project, I want each of you to discover why such strange foods are good for birds. Some of the answers are in the library. The rest might require field research."

"That's dumb," I whispered over to Amy. "What answers are we going to find in a field?"

"She just means you've got to look in places other than books and computers," Amy whispered back.

"Just kidding," I said. "I knew that. Hey, guess what? You should have seen the size of the raccoon that was eating our garbage last night — "

"Shhhh," Amy warned under her breath. "The teacher . . . "

I looked up. Miss Santos was staring at me.

"Kirby, what did I just tell the class?"

"Um . . . you said half of us will take home a bird-chow feeder, and the rest will take fatty bird cakes."

She nodded, then turned back to the class. "Set up your feeding stations at home. Over the next week, record the number and kind of birds that visit your feeders. Use good sketches and lots of description in your bird journals. It will be interesting to see which food the wild birds like best."

Jill raised her hand. "What bird journals?"

"The ones we are going to make right now. Back to your desks and take out your pencil crayons."

After school, I hung my bird-chow feeder in the apple tree outside the kitchen window. Then I sat at the kitchen table and waited. No birds came. I waited a little longer. Then I cranked open the window and called, "Here, birdie, birdie." Still no birds. Not even a butterfly. So I took out my red rocket yo-yo and practised "walk the dog" for a while. Still no birds.

Suddenly, I got an idea. I taped two sheets of paper together. In big, red letters, I printed:

KIRBY'S FLY-THRU RESTAURANT
Serving up delicious bird chow.
Don't be a dodo.
Eat here. It's free!

Underneath, I drew a picture of two cardinals

gobbling up bird chow. I stuck the sign in the apple tree so the birds would be sure to see it. Then I went back inside and waited. After a while, I saw some action. Leaves were rustling in the bushes at the back of our yard. I watched closely for a bird.

But instead of feathers, I saw fur — grey, brown and black fur.

Was that the raccoon? I wondered. And what was it doing in my backyard, in the day-time?

Chapter 5

One Strange Bird

Bird watching isn't much fun when there are no birds around. You just sit and stare at the trees, and watch the clouds drift by, and day-dream a little, and get hungry.

It was Saturday morning. I was sitting at the kitchen table, staring out the window at my lonely bird feeder. Dad was standing at the stove, flipping blueberry pancakes. I didn't notice it when he put a plate in front of me.

"Here you go, kiddo."

"Yes!" I shot my fist in the air. "It's about time, birdbrain!"

"Kirby!" Dad snapped. "That is no way to speak to your father!"

I started to laugh. Dad's eyebrows sank into a deep V.

"I was talking to a blue jay," I explained. "It just landed in the apple tree."

Dad messed up my hair, then walked over to the window. "That jay looks mighty hungry."

"I am, too," I said, turning to the plate in front of me. A line of berries smiled up at me. "Way to go, Dad. You made a happy-face pancake."

Dad wiped a blob of batter off his nose and smiled.

I used to think that blue jays were just blue. Now that I looked closely, I saw grey, white, black and *three* shades of blue. I picked up my journal and started to draw.

A few minutes later, five little birds flew up to the bird feeder, chirping and chattering, like they were best friends.

I looked at my pancake. My stomach growled. Oh, well, breakfast would have to wait. I started to sketch the chickadees.

When I finally got around to eating, the doorbell rang.

"Kirby," Dad called, "you have a visitor."

Amy, I thought. She's here early.

I stuffed the rest of the pancake in my mouth and ran. Miranda stood at the front door holding *my* puppy.

"This is Princess," she said. "Isn't she adorable? Don't you just love her golden curls?"

I wanted to grab the puppy and run. Instead, I wrinkled my nose and said, "Pyew! She smells."

Miranda hugged the puppy. "Princess does not smell!"

"Well, the air around here is getting pretty stinky."

"You're just jealous!"

"Why should I be? I'm getting my own dog. One that doesn't smell."

Miranda narrowed her eyes. "You're so jeal-ous, your hair is turning green!"

"Is not!"

"Is too. Go see for yourself!" She stormed off down the sidewalk with Princess.

I ran to look in the mirror. My hair was not green!

A few minutes later, the doorbell rang again. This time it was Amy.

"Hey, Kirbs, guess what? Two cardinals were pecking at my fatty bird cake this morning."

"Cardinals!" I exclaimed. "You're lucky!"

"One flew to the maple tree in your front yard when I crossed the street," Amy said.

"What are we waiting for?" I said. "Let's go get the feeder!"

We raced to the backyard, took the feeder down from the apple tree and ran back to the front of the house.

On the way, the grapefruit tipped, spilling bird chow on the driveway.

"Oops!" I said, slowing down. "Oh, well, there's still some left."

Our maple tree is taller than the apple tree. I inched my way up the trunk and hung the grapefruit on the bottom branch. "The cardinals can't miss it now," I called down to Amy.

"Birds are shy," Amy said. "They won't eat the bird chow if they see us."

So we hurried inside and waited by the living-room window.

"Guess what?" Amy said. "During reading, I found out why birds eat suet. Fat gives them energy to survive the cold winter."

"I read that, too!" I said. "And seeds are loaded with oil and vitamins."

"That was the easy part," Amy groaned. "What about dog bones and eggshells?"

I did a handstand on the carpet. "Mom took an injured crow to the wild bird rescue centre last year. Maybe we could ask them — "

"Kirbs . . . get over here! Quick!"

I flipped back onto my feet and ran to the window. "Whoa! That is one strange bird!"

I started to draw: Ears, short and sticking up straight. A long tail that nearly touched the ground. A raggedy coat of grey, brown, black and dirty white.

I grinned at Amy. "Miss Santos will be very surprised when she sees what's been eating my bird chow."

When I finished the picture, I pressed my nose to the window. "So you're the raccoon." Then I grabbed Amy's hand. "Let's go visit."

She pulled her hand back. "What if it's not friendly?"

"We'll take a couple of steps out the door," I said. "If it does anything scary, we'll run back inside."

"I guess so," Amy said slowly. "As long as we stay close to the house."

We tiptoed out the door. The bird-chow thief looked up. Its mouth was hanging open. Its long, pink tongue almost reached the ground.

"Let's go closer," I said.

"I don't know . . . "

We took two more steps. Without warning, the beast charged. Amy ran for the door, but the animal circled in front of her, blocking the way. She screamed and ran down the side-walk.

That rascal ran after her!

Chapter 6

My Dog Is Better Than Your Dog

"**H**ere, puppy!"

The dog stopped chasing Amy and scooted over to me. *Sniff, sniff, sniff* . . . Boy, he sure liked the smell of my shoes. And when I put my hand out, he licked me.

"The dog is friendly," I called to Amy. "He was just playing tag with you."

Amy peered around a tree. "Are you sure? I

don't know about dogs. But I do know that a hamster would never chase a kid. It would run the other way."

The dog followed me over to Amy. She froze like a Popsicle while he sniffed her shoes.

Then someone called to us. "Hey, wait up!"

It was Miranda. Princess was dangling from her arms.

"So you really did get a dog," she said when she'd caught up. "Wow, I thought you were kidding."

"Huh? A dog? Oh, you mean *this* dog. Yeah, um . . . he just got here."

Amy shot me a look. I pretended not to notice.

"Where did you get him from?" Miranda wanted to know.

"My parents sent for him," I told her, "from . . . the snowy mountains in . . . Quebec!"

Miranda stared at the dog, then at me. "That doesn't look like a mountain dog. What kind of breed is it?"

"A rare mix," I answered.

"Oh, you mean a mutt." She smirked. "Does he have a name?"

"A name? It's . . . uh . . . Rags! 'Cause his fur is all raggedy. That's his style."

"That's not a style. His coat is just messy."

"Your dog may be prettier," I snapped, "but my dog is smarter."

"Princess starts puppy school in one week. I'll bet that mutt never went to school."

"Rags is naturally smart," I said.

"He doesn't look smart. What can he do?"

"Tricks. You know, stuff like 'roll over.' "

Miranda's eyes narrowed. "What else?"

"Uh . . . he can catch a Frisbee in the air."

She lifted one eyebrow. "Really?"

"Sure! And that's not all. You should see him balance a ball on his nose — like a seal."

I glanced over at Amy. Her mouth was hanging wide open.

"Wow!" Miranda exclaimed.

"And walk on his hind legs . . . on a tightrope . . . ten metres above the ground."

Miranda's eyes completely bugged out. For

once, she couldn't beat me!

I grinned, showing all my teeth. "Can your dog do any of those tricks?"

"Well, no," she admitted. "She's still a baby."

"So there. My dog is smarter than your dog."

Miranda stood there, tapping her foot on the sidewalk. Suddenly, the tapping stopped. "Liar!" she roared. "You just got that dog. You couldn't have taught him those tricks. It's impossible."

I bit my lip. Think fast, think fast, think fast!

"I . . . I didn't have to teach him any tricks. He used to work . . . in a mountain circus."

I looked at Amy. She looked the other way.

"Prove it!" Miranda demanded. "Make him do the tricks."

"You mean here? Now?"

"Prove it, or I'll tell everyone you're a big, fat liar!"

I looked her straight in the eye. "I will prove it. Later. But right now, Rags needs to rest. He had a long trip."

Rags started to sniff the air. He followed his nose over to Miranda and jumped up on her legs.

"Ew! Your dog is getting dirt on my new jeans."

"It's not his fault," I said. "He smells your dog."

"My dog does not smell!" Miranda cried. "Your dog smells!"

Rags kept jumping up to visit Princess. The little pup barked and tried to wiggle out of Miranda's arms.

"Come on, Princess," Miranda said. "Let's get out of here." With a loud huff, she turned and stormed off.

Amy shook her head slowly. "*Why* did you tell Miranda that junk?"

"Did you hear the way she was putting down Rags? Someone had to stick up for him. Besides, she brought her puppy to my house this morning. To make me jealous! And you know what? It worked." I sank down onto the grass. "Just look at the mess I've made!"

I hid my face in my hands. A hot tear trickled down my cheek.

Then Rags tickled my fingers with his wet nose, making me laugh.

I lifted my hands off my face. "Peekaboo."

Rags put a dirty paw on my knee. Suddenly, things didn't seem so bad.

"Maybe my parents will let me keep Rags. Maybe I can train him to do all those tricks."

Amy shook her head again. "Kirbs, you're going to need some kind of wonder dog!"

Chapter 7

A Surprise Visitor

My family sat down to Sunday dinner. Mom popped a Brussels sprout in her mouth and went, "Mmmmmm."

"Nice try, Mom," I said. "But it won't work. Marcus isn't going to eat the Brussels sprouts."

Dad cut a pork chop into tiny pieces for Marcus. One by one, Marcus picked up the chunks of meat and shoved them into his mouth. He didn't chew and he didn't swallow.

He ate like a chipmunk, storing his food in his cheeks.

I turned away. I couldn't watch.

"Guess what?" I said to Mom and Dad. "After church, I phoned the wild bird rescue centre. The woman there told me why eggshells are good for birds. They're loaded with calcium — like milk — so they build strong bones. But that's not all: they're good for a bird's gizzard."

Mom and Dad didn't have a clue, so I explained: "Gizzard is a fancy name for bird guts. Since a bird has no teeth to chew its food, the gizzard does the job. It's a muscle that churns like a little blender in a bird's stomach. Birds eat tiny stones and gravel to help the gizzard grind up the food. But when snow covers the ground, stones are hard to find."

"I get it," Mom said. "Eggshells take the place of stones."

"Weird, eh?" I said.

"I was thinking," Dad said, "perhaps we could build a wooden bird feeder for the coming winter. That way . . . " His voice trailed off.

We froze in our chairs, listening to a *scrrratch . . . scrrrratch . . . scrrrratch* coming from our back door.

Mom touched her finger to her lips. "Do you think it's the raccoon?" she whispered.

Dad scratched his chin. "Hmmm . . . It would be very bold to come right up to the door."

Mom got up and grabbed the broom from the closet. The rest of us followed. She peered out the little window in the door.

"Well, I'll be . . . It's a dog!"

Marcus tried to climb up Dad's leg. "Me see! Me see!"

Dad lifted Marcus up to the window.

"That's odd," Dad said. "Why would a dog be scratching at our door?"

"I guess he likes our house," I offered.

Mom leaned against the broom. "Look. He's wearing a collar and tags. The dog must have a home."

"But Mom, his fur is all raggedy. He's mostly skin and bones. No one cares about him!"

Rags scratched at the door again.

"We can't just leave the poor thing like this," Mom said. "I'll go out and see if I can read his tags."

Mom opened the door. The broom she had been leaning on crashed to the floor. Rags shot straight up into the air, then ran off.

Marcus went stiff in Dad's arms. "Me want doggy! Me want doggy!" His face turned red. His eyes bulged. His cheeks were still full of meat — and they looked like they could go *kapow!* at any moment.

Mom and Dad carried Marcus upstairs to calm him down.

"Way to go, Marcus!" I cheered quietly. "Perfect timing." I picked up my plate from the kitchen table. "Here, Rags," I called out the back door.

He must have liked that name because he came running out of the darkness, right up to me. I held out my plate and he gobbled up the

pork chop and the rice. But he spit out the Brussels sprouts.

"That's okay," I said. "I don't like Brussels sprouts either."

I gave him a good scratch under the chin. "I'm really sorry," I told him, "but my parents won't let me keep you. So you have to go away."

Woof! Woof!

"Okay, you win. One more piece of meat. Then you have to go, or else I'll get in big trouble."

I turned around — and Mom was standing at the kitchen door. She came outside with her arms tightly folded. "Kirby, what are you doing?"

"Saying goodbye to Rags."

She threw her arms in the air. "Rags? You've given that dog a name. You're feeding him your dinner. And I'm supposed to believe that you're saying goodbye?"

"It's true, Mom. Why don't you believe me?"

Mom answered me with a stern look. Then she called softly, "Come here, little dog. Let me see your tags."

But Rags remembered Mom — she was the broom lady. His tail slipped between his legs, and he disappeared into the dark and lonely night.

Chapter 8

Big Trouble

When I woke up the next morning, I looked out my bedroom window. Some branches in the bushes out back had been flattened. Could it have been — ? I got dressed and ran outside.

Yes! It was Rags. He looked so cold and hungry and all alone.

"Don't worry," I told him, warming him with a hug. "I'll make you a nice little home."

Rags gave me a sloppy lick on the cheek.

Before long, I was so busy taking care of him that I forgot it was Monday. Then Amy knocked at the door.

"Did your parents let you keep Rags?" she asked.

"I'm working on it," I told her. "He came to visit me last night, but my parents were in a bad mood because of Marcus."

On the way to school, Amy and I dodged the cracks in the sidewalk as we chanted:

Step on a crack,
You're a maniac;
Step on a line,
You're Frankenstein.

A couple of times we stepped on the cracks on purpose, so we could pretend we were monsters and maniacs.

"Guess what?" Amy said as she hopped. "Miranda and I found out why dog bones are good for birds."

"You . . . and Miranda? How?"

"We read the list of ingredients on Princess's box of Puppy Treats. They're made with whole-wheat flour, meat, cheese, fat and corn — all good stuff."

I landed on a crack. "When were you at Miranda's?"

"Sunday afternoon."

"Why?"

"She asked me."

I clenched my fists. "How could you? After all the mean things she's done to me?"

Amy rolled her eyes. "If you two would just quit this crazy fight, maybe we could all be friends again."

"No way! Not after — " I stopped. Something cold and wet was touching the back of my leg. "Hey, look who sneaked up."

Rags gave Amy's hand a big, wet lick.

"See," I said. "He likes you."

"I like him, too. But I don't like this!" She dangled a wet hand in front of my face.

"EW! Dog drool!" we cried together.

Then Jared rode up beside us on his bike. "Hey, Kirby, is that your dog?"

I gave a quick nod.

"Here we go again," Amy said under her breath.

"Miranda says he can do amazing tricks. Can I see them?"

"Rags can't do his tricks now," I explained. "He needs special equipment — like ropes and balls."

"He doesn't have to do the fancy stuff," Jared said. "Just something easy, like 'roll over' or 'speak.' "

"Not now," I insisted.

"Why not?"

" 'Cause . . . it'll ruin the surprise."

"What surprise? Come on, Kirby, you can tell me."

"Oh, all right, if you must know . . . In a couple of days, Rags is going to star in a big show. Everyone is invited."

"What?" Amy blurted out.

"Awesome!" Jared shouted. He popped a wheelie. "Can I bring my cousin? He lives in Toronto."

"Sure," I said. "Why not?" I bit my bottom

lip. Oh, why did I open my big mouth?

"Wow," Jared exclaimed, "I can't wait to tell everyone." Before I could tell him to keep it a secret, he tore off.

"Now what are you going to do?" Amy asked. "Everyone is going to expect a circus show starring Wonder Dog."

I shrugged. "Teach Rags the tricks, I guess. How hard can that be?"

She shook her head. "If you're lucky, maybe Rags already knows some tricks."

"That's it! He looks smart." I got Rags' attention and said, "Sit."

Rags sat.

"Yahooooo! Rags is amazing! He can sit."

Even Amy had to smile. "That's good. Try another."

"Roll over."

Woof!

I tried again. "Roll over."

Rags sat.

"Do you think 'sit' is good enough?" I asked Amy.

"I think you're in big trouble," she answered.

I had no idea how big the trouble was until later at school.

Miranda stood up at Sharing Time and told the whole class about Rags.

Miss Santos leaned back in her desk and folded her arms. "Hmmm . . . I have never heard of a pet dog that could perform such difficult tricks."

"Rags worked at a circus before he was Kirby's dog," Miranda explained.

"Is that correct, Kirby?"

I bit the inside of my mouth and nodded.

"In that case, you must bring Rags to school, so the class can see these amazing tricks."

"No! I can't — I mean . . . I'm not sure if I'm allowed."

Amy raised her hand and tried her best to save me. "I can bring my hamster, Josephine. I'm allowed."

"That would be nice," Miss Santos said. "I

would like to meet Josephine." She turned back to me. "Kirby, I will phone your parents and invite Rags myself."

The teacher . . . phone my parents . . . about Rags?!

"NO! DON'T! I — I just remembered . . . I *am* allowed."

"Wonderful," Miss Santos said. "Tomorrow will be grade-three pet day. Kirby will bring her dog, and Amy will bring her hamster."

Miranda raised her hand. "May I bring my puppy? Her name is Princess."

"Sorry, Miranda," Miss Santos said. "I'm afraid two dogs in one classroom might cause problems. Princess may visit on another day."

Miranda shot me the evil eye.

If only she knew the truth: I would have given anything for Princess to trade places with Rags.

Chapter 9

Tricks 'n' Treats

After school, Amy came over to help me teach Rags amazing tricks.

Susan and Marcus were in the kitchen making chocolate-chip cookies.

"Isn't Marcus a good helper?" Susan said as she greased the cookie sheet. "He's big enough to mix the dough all by himself."

"Yeah, great," I said, reaching for a glass of water.

"Look," Amy whispered. "He's *eating* the dough."

I dropped my glass and yanked Marcus's hands out of the bowl. "Gross! Do you want the cookies to taste like dirty fingers?"

His face scrunched up.

"Quick, Amy," I warned, "let's get out of here. The little cookie monster is about to roar."

On our way out the door, I scooped up a wad of dough with my fingers. Yummy!

I took Amy to Rags' hideaway. He lay curled up on my pink baby blanket.

"I left five hot dogs on the blanket this morning," I told Amy. "Now, they're all gone. The poor dog must have been starving. No wonder he broke into our garbage."

"What if your parents find out?" Amy asked.

"They won't. Ever since that night when Mom scared Rags with the broom, he's been afraid to go near the back door — unless, of course, I'm there. Anyway, I *am* going to tell them."

"When?"

"Later — when the time is right."

Rags stretched himself out and wagged his tail.

"Ring! Ring!" I sang out. "Time for dog school."

"Kirbs, are you sure you need to do this?" Amy asked. "If you just tell Miss Santos the truth, I think she'll understand."

"No, it's too late. I'm too deep in this mess."

"Okay," she said, "but don't say I didn't warn you."

"Yeah, yeah, I know. Let's get started."

"Well, I was thinking," Amy said, "Rags doesn't understand words. Maybe if we demonstrate the tricks — "

I knocked myself on the head. "Why didn't I think of that?"

"I'm teacher," Amy said. "Called it."

"Okay. I wanted to be the dog anyway." I dropped onto my hands and knees and barked.

"Roll over," Amy commanded, trying not to laugh.

I rolled over. Rags wagged his tail.

"Now it's your turn, Rags," Amy said. "Roll over."

Rags wagged his tail.

I rolled over again. And again! Rags thought I was playing. He pounced and licked my ear.

"Stop!" I cried. "This isn't a game."

His tail dropped between his legs.

"It's okay," I said, petting him. "We'll start with an easier trick."

I ran to the shed and dug around until I found my Frisbee. "Fetch," I shouted, tossing the disc through the air.

Rags sat!

"Try taping cheese to the Frisbee," Amy said. "I'll bet Rags would like that."

"You know, for someone who doesn't know about dogs, you're pretty smart," I told her. Then I ran to the kitchen and got some smelly blue cheese and a roll of tape.

Now Rags was interested. He started dancing on his hind legs, trying to bite at the cheese.

I let the Frisbee fly again. "Fetch!"

Rags started running. *Woof! Woof!*

The Frisbee began to glide back down to earth.

Woof! Woof! Woof!

"Jump, Rags, jump!" we cried. "Now!"

But Rags didn't jump. He sat. And he didn't budge until the Frisbee landed in the garden. Then he tore off, grabbed the cheese and ran with it.

"Cheater!" I kicked the ground. "Oh, what's the use?"

"Don't give up," Amy said. "So what if Rags can't roll over or catch a Frisbee? Those aren't the big tricks anyway."

I groaned. "If you say so."

When I brought my red ball out of my backpack, Rags started to wiggle.

"Uh-oh," Amy said. "He wants to chase the ball."

I held the ball in place on his nose and said, "Stay still." Slowly, I let go of the ball.

With a toss of his head, Rags sent the ball flying through the air. Away he ran after it. He brought it back and dropped it in front of me, begging me to throw it again.

"No! I'm not playing fetch."

Rags nudged the ball closer to my feet with his nose.

"This stinks!" I growled. "If a seal can balance a ball on its pointy nose, why can't you?"

"Try the biggest and best trick," Amy said. "If he can learn that, it'll make everyone forget about the rest." She opened her backpack and pulled out a skipping rope. "*Voilà!* A tightrope."

We each grabbed an end of the rope and stretched it out close to the ground. That way even if Rags fell, he wouldn't get hurt.

Rags wasn't interested in the skipping rope. So we wiggled it in front of his nose. Suddenly, he snapped it up in his mouth, tearing it from our hands. He started running in circles, shaking the skipping rope and growling.

"Look," Amy said, pointing. "Rags thinks he's fighting a snake."

Rags tossed the snake into the air — and

when it landed, he pounced.

Amy and I fell down laughing.

"What a brave dog!" Amy cried. "Fighting a skipping rope."

Susan came running outside. "What's all the racket about?"

Rags dropped the skipping rope and pranced over to her.

"Hi, fella," she said.

Rags put his paws in the air, begging. Susan laughed. "I'll bet you smell the cookies," she said. "So, Kirby, whose dog is this?"

Yikes! "Hers," I said, pointing to Amy.

"Oh, how nice," Susan said. She got down on one knee to pet Rags. He licked her back. "He's really friendly," she said, wiping her face with the back of her hand. "Well, I'd better get back to the kitchen. The cookies are ready to come out of the oven."

Amy shot me an angry look.

"Dog school is a bust," I said to her. "Let's go chow down."

Amy grabbed her backpack and started to

walk away. "I'm not hungry."

"But chocolate-chip cookies are your favourite treat!"

She planted her fists on her hips. "It's bad enough that you lied to Susan. But did you have to make me a part of your lie?"

"I didn't mean to! It all happened so fast — I didn't know what to say. Amy, I'm sorry. I'll fix everything. Promise."

She went home anyway. "You'd better," she said over her shoulder.

That night I couldn't sleep. I had to think of something — and fast! Time was running out.

Maybe Rags and I could run away and join a circus. But then I would miss my friends and family. Suddenly, I got a better idea — a way out of this mess. The problem was I'd have to tell one more lie. A whopper!

Chapter 10

Rags Goes to School

The next morning I got up extra early. I had tons to do before school.

In Mom's sewing drawer, I found a piece of blue satin — the perfect size for a little cape. With my gold glitter glue, I wrote "WONDER DOG" on the satin.

Next I searched the bathroom closet and found a long, stretchy bandage — the kind Dad wraps around his sore knee when he plays hockey.

Rags was asleep on his blanket when I arrived with the first-aid supplies. "Wake up, sleepyhead," I called softly.

His tail thumped on the blanket.

"Hold still," I told him. "This won't hurt a bit."

Carefully, I wound the cloth around his left front leg, making sure it was not too tight and not too loose. Then I fastened it with a metal clip — just the way Dad does it.

Rags bit at the cloth, then looked up at me with sad eyes.

"It's only for a little while," I tried to explain.

When I walked back into the house, Amy was knocking on the front door with her knee. Her arms were wrapped around Josephine's cage.

"Bye, Susan," I called up the stairs.

"Bye, Kirby," she answered. "Have a nice day."

Amy followed me to the backyard. Then she saw Rags. "What happened?" she gasped.

"Promise you won't tell?"

"What did you do this time?"

I explained my plan.

Amy shook her head and spoke slowly. "Now you've gone too far."

"But how else can I get myself out of this mess?"

She didn't answer.

"Don't be mad," I begged. "This is the *last* lie. Promise. *Pinkie swear.*"

A little smile crept onto her lips. We locked our baby fingers together. "Remember, Kirbs," she said. "A promise is a promise."

Reaching into my backpack, I pulled out the satin cape. "Ta-da!" I tied the two front ends around Rags' neck.

"At least Rags looks like a wonder dog," Amy said, "even if he doesn't act like one."

Sniff, sniff, sniff . . . Rags smelled Josephine. He pawed at the cage.

"Down, Rags." Amy raised the cage over her head.

"This crazy dog needs a leash," I said, pulling him back.

"Get my skipping rope," Amy said. "Hurry, my arms are getting sore."

Reaching into Amy's backpack, I pulled out the skipping rope and tied it around Rags' collar.

When we reached the school, Amy took Josephine straight to the classroom. Rags and I walked around the schoolyard, waiting for the bell. Some kids from my class came running up.

"What happened to your dog?" Craig asked, pointing to the bandage.

"He broke his leg," I answered.

"How?" Jill wanted to know.

Rats! I hadn't thought about that! My brain was turning to mush.

Just in time, I came up with a good one: "Rags was practising for the big show when BOOM! — he fell off the tightrope."

Jill put her hand over her mouth. "Oh, my gosh! How high was the rope?"

"This high," I said, reaching my hand over my head.

"That's awful," Miranda said. "I would hate

it if anything bad ever happened to Princess."

"Can he still do his tricks?" Jared wanted to know.

"NO," I said in a loud voice, so everyone would hear. "Rags will never be able to perform his tricks again."

"But," Jared began, "my cousin's coming from Toronto to — "

Ring! Ring! Ring!

Whew! Saved by the bell. I took a deep breath and headed into school.

Miss Santos was sitting at her desk when I got to class. "Very pretty cape, Rags," she said. "I'll bet someone special made that for you."

I lifted his bandaged leg. "Rags is hurt," I said. "He won't be able to perform his tricks."

"What a shame," Miss Santos said. "Could he show us a few easy ones?"

"I guess so," I mumbled.

After morning announcements, Miss Santos called Rags and me to the front of the class.

Jared gave me thumbs-up. Amy covered her eyes.

"You may begin," Miss Santos said.

"Sit!" I commanded.

Rags sat.

Everyone clapped. Then the room went quiet — and my face went red.

"Is that all?" Miss Santos asked, finally.

"Yes," I said. "The other tricks might hurt his leg."

Miss Santos gave me a strange look. "All right, Kirby, take Rags back to your desk." She called Josephine to the front of the room.

Amy took Josephine out of her cage. "This is my pet hamster. She is one year old. Her name is Josephine. She can run in a ball."

Then she brought a clear ball out of her backpack. With a twist of her wrist, the ball came apart into two pieces. Amy put Josephine inside, then snapped the two parts back together. She put the ball on the floor. Josephine started running. The ball rolled across the room.

"Wow!" Craig exclaimed, hanging off the side of his desk. "That is one speedy hamster!"

Rags watched the ball roll down the aisle. He started to whimper. Then the ball rolled past his nose. He smelled Josephine. I felt a tug on the skipping rope.

A ball and a hamster. Together. Trouble for any dog!

Woof! Woof!

"Shhhh, Rags!"

Woof! Woof! Woof! Rags pulled on the skipping rope. The knot around his collar started to slip. I reached out to grab the collar. At the same time, the ball bumped into his paws. Rags lunged. The knot came undone, and he took off after Josephine.

The class cheered: "Go Josephine! Go Josephine!" Josephine's strong little legs rolled the ball between the desks. Rags caught up, pawed the ball — then Josephine sped away.

"Stop that dog!" Miss Santos ordered.

Amy crawled under a desk and rescued Josephine.

Half the class helped me chase Rags. He ran

faster than all of us, sprinting in circles around the room.

And then it happened: the bandage started to unravel. A long, white streak trailed behind Rags.

I froze.

"Faker!" Jared shouted. "That dog didn't break his leg!"

Rags tore by Jill's desk. She reached out and grabbed his collar. "Gotcha!"

Miss Santos smoothed her hair back into place. She walked to the front of the class. "Kirby," she said firmly, "is there something you would like to say to the class?"

Gulp. Now what was I going to do? Here I was, caught in the biggest lie of my life — in front of the whole class.

One more lie could get me out of this mess, I told myself. One more itty-bitty lie.

Chapter 11

Friends to the Rescue

The class sat waiting for me to speak, but I couldn't come up with anything. It was a bad time for my brain to go on the blink. I couldn't think fast, and I couldn't think straight. Then it hit me. I knew the reason why: I'd made a promise to Amy.

Not just any old promise. The pinkie-swear kind.

I walked back to my desk and didn't look at

anyone. Still, I could feel everyone's eyes on me.

"Kirby?" Miss Santos said. "We're waiting."

Don't cry, don't cry, I told myself. It didn't work. My chin started to quiver. Tears streamed down my face. "R-Rags isn't mine," I blubbered. "He's a s-s-tray, and the only trick he knows is 'sit.' "

"Oh, dear," Miss Santos said. "Kirby, step into the hall at once. The rest of the class, read quietly at your desks."

Miss Santos stood in the hall with her hands on her hips and a frown on her face.

My chin started to quiver again. "Sorry, I lied," I said. "I — I wanted a dog so-o-o bad. That's all. Now I've ruined everything. Everyone's going to h-h-hate me."

Miss Santos put her arm around my shoulder. "Maybe they'll forgive you," she said. "After all, everyone makes mistakes, and you did tell the truth — eventually."

I bent down to pet Rags.

"Kirby," Miss Santos said, "Rags has a collar and dog tags. That means he belongs to someone. Do your parents know about this?"

"Yes . . . No . . . I mean, I'm going to tell them tonight."

"Good," she said. "For now, tie up Rags at the back of the school. He'll be safe there."

"Miss Santos, my stomach feels sick. May I go home?"

"And miss the results of our wild bird project?"

"Oh, yeah, I forgot."

When I made it back to class, I heard whispering and giggling. I still couldn't look at anyone — not even Amy. For the rest of the morning, I stared at the ink spot on my desk.

At recess, I dashed out of the classroom.

"Wait up!" a voice called behind me.

I kept running — straight to Rags. Amy and Jill finally caught up. "Are you okay?" Amy asked. "That was so hard . . . you know . . . what you did in class."

"I feel so dumb," I said, resting my head on Rags' neck. He put his paw in my hand.

"Amy told me why you lied," Jill said. "Don't

worry, I'm not mad at you. It was mostly Miranda's fault."

"Miranda didn't make me lie," I said. "I did that all by myself."

Then Jared walked by, grinning. "Hey, Kirby, want to come over after school and meet my pet elephant? You should see the amazing tricks she can do."

"Ignore him," Jill said.

"Oh, no," I groaned, "look who's coming." I buried my face in Rags' fur.

Amy stood in front of me as Miranda approached. "Leave Kirby alone," she told her. "She doesn't want to talk to you."

Miranda stepped back. "But . . . I just — "

I lifted my head. "Miranda, I don't want to fight any more. You win. You got Princess. And I'm just a big, fat liar."

I thought that would make her happy, but do you know what? She looked miserable. Slowly, she turned and walked away.

So after all that, Miranda and I were both miserable. Maybe, in the end, nobody had won.

Chapter 12

And the Winner Is . . .

"Class, it is time for us to look at the results of our experiment. I want each student to stand and give a report." Miss Santos stood by the blackboard, ready to keep score.

When it was my turn, I stood and called out, "Four blue jays, twelve black-capped chickadees, seven starlings, one squirrel, and — " I opened my journal to the sketch of Rags — "here's proof that dog bones really are for dogs."

Craig piped up. "Rags really is a wonder dog! I mean, you have to wonder about a dog that eats *eggshells*."

Everyone cracked up.

"All eyes to the blackboard," Miss Santos said. When the class was quiet, she announced the final score. "Four hundred seventy-one birds ate fatty bird cake and 237 birds ate bird chow. She nodded to the class. "Drum roll, please!"

The thunder of fingers beating on desks filled the room.

"And the winner is . . . "

"Fatty bird cake!" the class shouted.

After school, I walked Rags home and tied him out back. Dad arrived home before Mom. I told him everything.

He dropped onto the living-room chair. "The city is a dangerous place for a lost dog," he said. "Rags could get run over, or into a dogfight, or picked up by the dog catcher."

"Rags isn't lost," I insisted. "I've found him.

And once he moves into our house, he'll be safe. I'll take good care of him. Promise."

Dad shook his head. "You know, Kirby, Rags probably has a family of his own. What if they're looking for him right now?"

"You don't understand, Dad. Rags is happy. He *picked* me."

Dad took my hand and gave it a little squeeze. "I'm going to phone City Hall before it closes," he said. "It's the right thing to do."

"*Oh* . . . all right, but if no one has reported a lost dog, can I keep him? Can I, can I? Huh, huh? . . . OH, PLEEEEEASE!"

"Kirby, go and copy down Rags' licence number."

"But Dad — "

"Now."

I copied down "1725" on a scrap of paper and gave it to Dad. He went into the den and closed the door behind him. I heard mumbling, then the click of the phone being hung up.

Dad came out and wrapped his big arms around me. "The dog's name is Fergus. He's been missing for three weeks. City Hall is going to contact the owners right away."

"No! It's a mistake!" I cried, tearing myself from his arms.

I sat at the living-room window and watched the cars go by. An hour passed, and no one came to get Rags. Just like I thought. It was a mistake.

But then a blue minivan pulled up in our driveway. A girl about my age, with long, brown hair like mine, got out of the back. She and her mother walked up to the door. Dad brought Rags around to the front of the house.

"Fergus!" the girl cried. "I've missed you."

Rags . . . Fergus — whatever! — started to bark and jump all over the girl.

She walked up to me and smiled. "Hi, I'm Sarah. Thanks for taking care of my dog. I've been *so* worried."

Her mother shook my hand. "We'd like to give you a reward for returning Fergus to us safely." She held out a ten dollar bill.

Without warning, my eyes went blurry. I ran to my bedroom.

A little while later, Mom knocked on my door. Marcus came barrelling in after her. "I just got home," she said. "Dad told me what happened. Are you all right?"

I lifted my head off the bed. "It's not fair! I miss Rags."

Mom stroked my hair. "Rags will miss you too. But he's back with his real family now. And they love him as much as you do."

"Now I'll never get a dog of my own. Marcus will never grow up."

"I am growed up," Marcus said. He pulled up his shirt and stuck out his tummy. "See?"

Mom laughed. "You know, Kirby, one year will make a big difference."

I sat straight up. "Mom, don't joke. Are you saying I can get a dog next year?"

"Yes. That is what I mean."

Marcus jumped on the bed. "Me too! Me too!"

I wrestled him down. "She means both of us, silly."

Marcus and I leaped off the bed and danced around the room.

Mom pulled the ten dollar bill from her pocket. "Fergus's family wanted you to have this. Why don't you buy yourself something special?"

"Maybe . . . " I said, catching my breath. "Amy's hamster is pretty cool."

The next day at the pet shop, Mom and Dad headed straight for the hamster section. But I spotted something else. Something wonderful. I turned down a different aisle.

"Come see," I called. "She's beautiful. She has soft, white fur and she's licking me right through the cage."

Mom and Dad marched over, dragging Marcus behind them.

"Kirby," Mom said in a tired voice, "we've told you a million times: no dogs!"

"It's not a dog," I said. "It's a rat."

"Oh, in that case — *what?* Did you say *rat?*"

"Just look at her long, scaly tail," I said. "And those beady red eyes. Isn't she cute? Don't you just love her? And look, she only costs eight ninety-nine. I can pay for her with my reward money."

Mom and Dad didn't answer. They couldn't. Their mouths were stuck open.

The pet shop owner walked over. "May I help you?"

"Yes. I would like a rat."

"Excellent choice," he said. "Rats make good pets. They're very gentle. Smart, too!"

I punched the air. "Yes! I'll build my rat a maze. I'll teach it daring tricks. And I'll invite my friends to an amazing show . . . starring Super Rat! Mom? Dad? Say something!"

That afternoon, Miranda and Princess came to my door.

"I'm sorry. About the dog . . . and everything," Miranda said. "I've been acting really dumb."

"Me too," I said. "Who's ever heard of a dog that could walk on a tightrope?"

We both laughed.

She took the green rocket yo-yo out of her

pocket. "Trade you. I know the green was your favourite."

"That's okay," I said. "I've decided I like the red one."

We looked at each other and smiled.

"Want to take Princess for a walk?" Miranda asked. "You can hold the leash."

"Awesome," I said. "But first I want to show you something." I pointed to the lump moving around in my shirt.

Miranda jumped back. "Yikes! Is it a snake?"

"Even better." I pulled out Rosie. "It's a rat."

Her eyes grew large. "Wow! I've never seen a rat that colour. Can I hold her?"

I put Rosie in Miranda's hands. She crawled up her arm and under her shirt. Miranda wiggled. "Rosie sure is friendly. Can she come for a walk too?"

"Why not?" I said. "She can ride on your shoulders."

While Miranda played with Rosie, I went outside and gave Princess a hug. "Remember me, Fuzzy-Wuzzy?"

Princess looked up at me with those big, brown eyes . . . and sank her teeth into my arm.

I shook a finger at her. "When are you ever going to learn? I am *not* a chew toy!"

Then a voice came from behind us. "Oh, no! Princess? What are you doing here?"

I looked up. Amy was standing over me. "Kirbs, you didn't . . . did you? Come on, we have to take Princess home right away!"

I just laughed.

Miranda stepped out onto the porch with Rosie on her shoulder.

"I give up!" Amy cried. "What's going on?"

"Miranda and I are friends again," I explained as I untied Princess. "And the rat is mine. Her name is Rosie."

"Ready to go for a walk?" Miranda asked us.

"Okay. But first, let's stop at my house and get Josephine," Amy said. "I can't wait for her to meet Rosie."

Woof! Woof! Princess lunged forward.

"Hold on!" I cried, pulling back on the leash.

Miranda grinned. "She still has eight weeks

of puppy school left — and she needs it!"

Princess lunged again.

"Uh-oh," Amy laughed. "Ready or not — Princess is taking you for a walk!"

"In that case," I said, "what are we waiting for? Let's go-o-o-o — !"

The idea for writing this book came naturally to **Beverly Scudamore**: as a kid, she could never pass a stray dog or cat without trying to bring it home. Twice, she actually convinced her parents to let her keep a stray.

Today, Beverly is the proud owner of her own "wonder dog": a springer spaniel named Kaily, whose tricks include sliding down a playground slide and singing at the piano.

This is Beverly's second Shooting Star novel. She and her family live in Bright's Grove, Ontario.